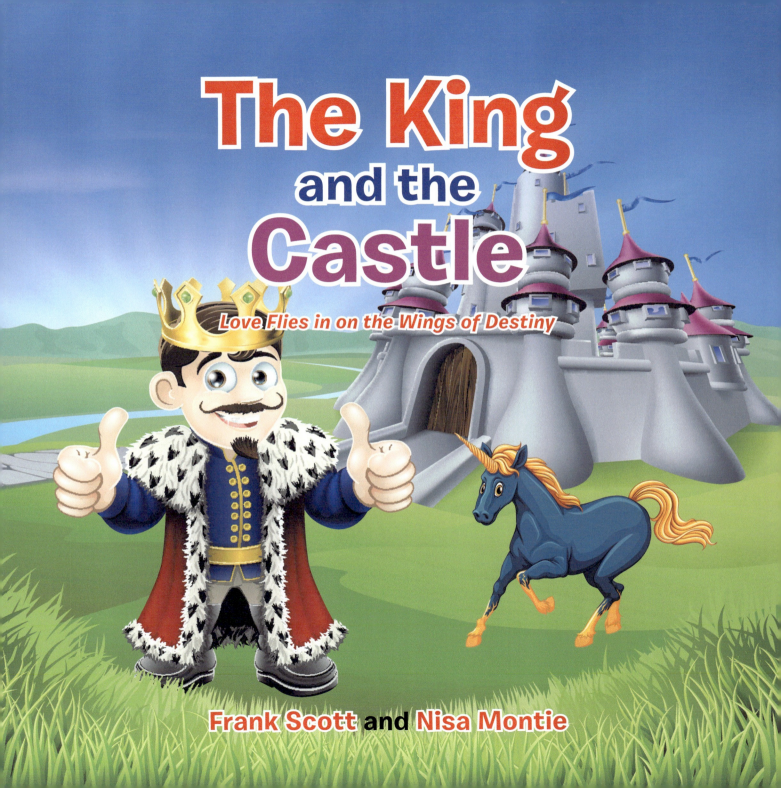

The King
and the
Castle

Love Flies in on the Wings of Destiny

Frank Scott and **Nisa Montie**

Balboa Press books may be ordered through booksellers or by contacting:

Balboa Press
A Division of Hay House
1663 Liberty Drive
Bloomington, IN 47403
www.balboapress.com
1 (877) 407-4847

Because of the dynamic nature of the Internet, any web addresses or links contained in this book may have changed since publication and may no longer be valid. The views expressed in this work are solely those of the author and do not necessarily reflect the views of the publisher, and the publisher hereby disclaims any responsibility for them.

Any people depicted in stock imagery provided by Thinkstock are models, and such images are being used for illustrative purposes only.
Certain stock imagery © Thinkstock.

ISBN: 978-1-5043-4354-1 (sc)
ISBN: 978-1-5043-4355-8 (e)

Print information available on the last page.

Balboa Press rev. date: 10/26/2015

BALBOA.
PRESS
A DIVISION OF HAY HOUSE

Table of Contents

Impetuous

Once upon a time there was a young Prince who had no family, having lost both his parents. He was rather wealthy and lived in a big house with a couple of servants, but knew something was still missing in his life. Before his mother died, she said,

"Leon, you have a special destiny. If you have not found your purpose for being here on Earth by the time you are twenty-five, you would do well to go on a quest to find your *true* kingdom and castle."

Prince Leon was a bit beyond his twenty-fifth year, yet he'd been putting off venturing outside his childhood home.

He was really a homebody, never having gone to overnight camp, and preferring to spend his days in his room reading fairy tales. For one thing, he was really bad at camping. The tent poles never seemed to line up right, making a fire was something he preferred to leave to the servants, the moldy leaves and grass caused him to sneeze, and hiking more than a quarter mile hurt his feet. So Leon decided to talk to the Almighty.

"God, would You please help me? Send me a sign that it is time to find my fortune, preferably with some stops at reputable inns.

As often happens when humans invoke the Divine, they soon forget the requests they have so fervently made.

That night, after a particularly challenging game of chess with his knight Bridget (Bridget won),

Leon went to bed and dreamed of nothing more than the winning chess moves he could have made with just a bit more time.

On awakening, just as dawn was breaking, with the birds singing mightily, he heard a pounding loud as a jack hammer on the outside of the wooden shutters. Since he slept on the second floor, he wondered what kind of giant pileated woodpecker could have mistaken the window coverings for a tree.

As the wooden shutters crashed open, an iridescent, turquoise-colored Unicorn landed before him. The Unicorn folded his wings, gazed at him with an emerald-green eye, and said,

"I have been sent in answer to your request." Leon sat up in his bed in his purple, polka-dotted, silk pj's.

"Oh," he said. He was just going to ask what his request had been when he remembered his prayer to the Creator. Then he noticed that one of his shutters hung dangling. "You broke my shutter. But that's OK," he added hastily, remembering that this Unicorn was sent from *On High*.

"My name is Impetuous. It is time to start your journey for your *kingdom and castle,*" declared the Unicorn, tossing his brilliant head and mane.

Leon was confused—had he really asked for this? Irritated at being woken up so early, he replied grumpily,

"How do you propose we do that?"

"Jump on my back!" Impetuous lowered his gleaming head. Leon looked warily at the slippery back. "Don't be concerned. You can hang onto my mane." Just then there was a knock at the door.

"What would you like for breakfast," called in Bridget, who, besides serving as his guard, brought his meals. Leon looked at the Unicorn.

"I have to step out for a bit," he called out through the closed door. "Would you mind packing me a lunch, please, Bridget?"

"No problem," said Bridget. Returning in a few minutes, she opened the door and handed Leon a bulging leather sack with a shoulder strap, and a flask of water. "Here you go. See you for dinner."

"Thank you very much," the Prince said as he took his lunch. The Unicorn, standing in the shadowed corner, went unnoticed.

"I'll send someone up to fix that shutter." Bridget exited, and Impetuous and Leon looked at each other with relief.

It would have been hard to explain the presence of a Unicorn. While waiting for his provisions, Leon had changed into sensible thick pants and boots, a comfortable shirt, and waterproof jacket with a hood. He felt quite outfitted.

"I'm ready to go," he told his new flying friend. Impetuous knelt down in a flash of gleaming color, and the Prince climbed onto his back.

Flight

Clinging to Impetuous' mane, Leon flew out the window. The pines and firs got tinier as the two new friends soared upwards, Leon's hair and the Unicorn's mane blowing in the wind.

As he watched the valley disappear beneath them, Leon relaxed on the Unicorn's back. Soon they approached some high mountains that seemed half-suspended in the blue-gray mist.

"Now listen up," Impetuous called out through the whooshing sound of his rising and falling wings. "When you feel that we are approaching your kingdom and castle, tap me on the shoulder and say, 'Impetuous, fly down there!' so that I will know to begin landing."

"Will do," Leon shouted back. For a moment, Leon closed his eyes. As he focused within, a tingling spread from his head to his entire body. Opening his eyes, he saw that they were approaching a large, clear body of water with a stand of pines on one side and an orchard on the other. Just beyond the orchard stood a gray, stone castle rising up from the land, as solid as if it had been planted there forever. Leon pounded on Impetuous' shoulder.

"Hey, watch it. I require my shoulder blades to fly. Is that the place?"

"Yes! That's it!" Leon told him. Impetuous grinned.

"All right. Hold on." They plunged down like an airplane that has lost its engines. His heart pounding loudly, Leon clutched the Unicorn's mane and watched as water, trees, and sandy shore rose up to meet them. As they landed next to the lake edged with cattails, ducks quacked and geese honked at their sudden arrival.

With an effort, the Prince stiffly pulled his leg over the Unicorn's back to slide down to Earth.

"Yes!" Leon said as he landed on the ground, then plopped down onto his stomach on the sun-warmed shore. Small waves lapped nearby. Relaxing into the sand, he thought about the amazing, air-borne trip.

"Excuse me. I'll be back in a minute." Impetuous trotted off to explore the stand of pines nearby. Leon took a deep breath and released it. He knew his life's adventure had now begun.

The Castle

The sun had risen much higher by the time the two friends were ready to continue their journey. Away they flew, over the lake and across a bright meadow filled with red poppies, asters, and Queen Anne's lace. A stone building appeared ahead of them. It was a large castle with turrets and golden flags flying. A bright, blue Unicorn leaping towards a crescent moon flapped on each of the flags that marked the corners of the castle walls. Surprised, Leon looked at Impetuous,

"You're on all the flags." The Unicorn smiled and quickened his pace as they galloped up to the castle walls.

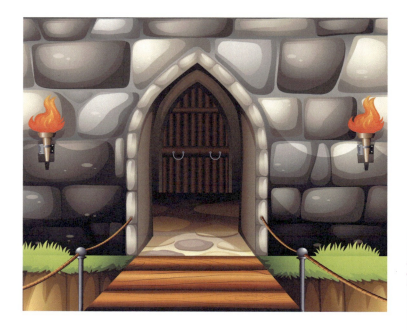

Two massive wooden doors fortified with iron bands faced them. All was quiet. Strangely, no guards greeted them.

A crow cawed three times. Above them, a falcon flew by on swift wings. Impetuous knelt down, and Leon slid off.

"Why don't you see if the door opens," said Impetuous. Leon grasped the giant, brass handle and pushed. Amazingly, the door opened easily.

"There's nothing here," Leon said quietly. The courtyard was empty: no chickens and pigs running around with servants chasing them, no children swinging leather balls on strings, or screaming with delight as they ran after and caught each other, and in the Great Hall, no minstrels harping and singing tales of heroes and heroines of old. The huge, stone fireplace sat cold and dark beyond the long, bare wooden tables.

"Where is everyone?" exclaimed Leon. He felt a sudden longing for his red, woolen cloak.

"They are waiting for the return of the magical age, when the Heart of the King is opened again like a red rose blossoming."

"What does that mean?" It was too much information. Leon thought of his cozy bed and supper.

"You will soon know." His turquoise Friend tossed his head and winked at him. "Let me tell you the story of the *Legend of the King....*

Once upon a time, there was a King who very much loved his Queen. Unfortunately, the Queen took an ill-advised journey during the Winter to visit her sick sister. On the way back by horseback, the Queen became chilled and feverish. The King called in the healers, but the Queen was not able to regain her strength. She left the Earthly plane.

The King could not accept the loss of his dearly beloved. His heart became filled with grief, anger, and bitterness. He could not rule justly or well, so he left on a journey, and the Kingdom foundered without its leader. The prophesy is that when the new King finds his Heart again through the love of strangers, he will return and rule once more.

The people will welcome him eagerly. Smells of cooking and the sounds of music and laughing children will emanate from the courtyard. Perhaps even a Queen will appear."

"Am I the King, then?" Leon asked, understanding and yet not understanding.

"That remains to be seen," replied Impetuous, flicking his tail.

Leon felt oppressed. Why was he being given such a big task, and how was he to accomplish it? Absentmindedly, he patted his chest. Then he laughed.

"My heart's all right. It's not such a big deal.

Let's go find the town and some strangers." He chuckled, and Impetuous bent down, saying,

"Yes! Let's paint the town—or whatever it is you humans say."

"Besides," noted Leon as he climbed onto the Unicorn's bright back, "I'm hungry."

God-Sent

Away from the empty castle, and over the forest, they flew. As they neared the edge of the trees, they heard the sounds of clattering hoofs, criers, and a general hullabaloo indicating a local market (*food*, thought Leon). Impetuous landed. They trotted across a wooden bridge spanning a lively stream, and headed into the sunlight of the village gathering place.

Leon was relieved to find people—old and young people bent over baskets and buckets of onions, potatoes, red chard, and even dried fish.

"I'm going to scout out some hay," Impetuous told Leon. "I'll be back soon."

Watching his friend move away, Leon felt a bit nervous. He did notice that the Unicorn's color seemed to have dimmed a bit and his horn had become translucent. At first glance, he seemed to be an oddly-colored stallion.

Two children rushed by in ragged clothing, knocking against Leon and throwing him off-balance.

"Hey!" he shouted, startled. A mother called out an apology. A villager of indeterminate age, dressed in buckskin dyed green, came up with a basket of apples. "How much?" asked Leon. He could have eaten almost anything by now.

"Pick one." The merchant held out the basket, and Leon chose a nice, big fruit. He rubbed it on his shirt and took a bite. Juicy!

"Thanks. This is yummy."

"You're welcome, Sire," she grinned. Then she was lost in the crowd before the Prince had time to react to the word *Sire*.

"Excuse me, Sir."

The Prince looked down and saw a child of four or five coming up to him. He wore a stained, light-colored shirt, blue pants, and held a bunch of lilies in his hand.

"A lady asked me to give this to you with this message,

`The Love that thou Art has no bounds. Embrace it.'"

The boy carefully placed the delicate flowers into the Prince's hands, then disappeared into the market throng. Leon looked at the flowers. Everything seemed to disappear but their delicate beauty. Just then Impetuous appeared, munching hay that stuck out of the corners of his mouth.

"Look," the Prince said as he carefully lifted up the flowers.

"Ah—*the First Sign.*"

"What?" Impetuous wouldn't say anything more except,

"Good hay. So crunchy and light. Almost makes up for the journey's wear-and-tear on my wings." Leon laughed as the two friends headed off to check out the rest of the marketplace.

An old man sat with an iron wheel that spun on two poles. Little marks were chiseled into its sides.

He sang out,

"Wheel of fate. Wheel of fate. I shall spin it. Stop it where you will. Know your destiny to fulfill. Wheel of fate."

"What do we do?" Leon asked, feeling awkward.

"*Wheel of fate. I shall spin it.* Stop it where you will." The old man held out his hand for payment. Without thinking, Leon handed him the lilies. The old man nodded and smiled. So Leon leaned close and did his best to see the little characters on the side before they disappeared in the whirling of the black circle.

"Stop!" he told the elder.

Immediately the old man grabbed the wheel with his hand, his pointer finger indicating a purple encoding. It looked like a "Y." Impetuous, who had been standing by quietly, tossed his brilliant mane and said,

"The Second Sign."

The seer, his eyes shining, turned towards the Prince.

"It means, Anointed One, that you have come to a fork in the road. One way is the familiar route of outward longings and inward sufferings. This is the way of the ego-mind. It is filled with careful plans, goals, and objectives. It gives the illusion of control, and security.

The second way is the unknown way of the *Mystery of Divine Love*. It can only be known each day with Faith at one's side. This second way frightens many people. The Heart, cast into the crucible of compassionate Oneness, the sea-depth of *Joy,* slowly opens like a ripe melon, its unknowable essence spilling out like sticky juice."

The old man turned back towards the iron circle.

Leon straightened up, un-hunching his shoulders. He looked at his Unicorn friend.

"Impetuous, I'm ready for the second way of the heart." A wave of happiness swept over both of them.

In a wild frenzy of pounding hoofs, tossing mane, swishing tail, and flying sparks of turquoise light, Impetuous starting dancing.

Leon leaped out of the way. But the energy was infectious. Laughing, he, too, began cavorting and twisting and dancing around the turquoise whirlwind that was the Unicorn. Suddenly, they both stopped, stood quietly, breathing hard, and looked at each other through the dust. Impetuous placed his sensitive nose on Leon's chest.

Music sounded. Looking around in surprise, they saw a boy about ten-years-old passing by, playing his flute. The Unicorn whisked his tail against the boy's back. The boy turned around.

"A Unicorn!" he exclaimed delightedly.

"Would you honor us with a Highland tune?" asked Impetuous politely.

"Certainly." The boy struck up a lively, joyous air.

"Whoopee," shouted Leon as he felt his feet beginning to dance again, and his arms beginning to swing. The boy was skipping and playing, Impetuous was snorting and stamping his hooves, and Leon felt as if he were a mountain stream bursting at last from its underground spring. People stared, laughed, and joined in the surging dance.

An old woman hobbled up. When Leon noticed her, his heart filled with compassion as he remembered his own mother at that age. "May I have this dance?" he asked, gallantly holding out his hands. The old woman smiled warmly.

"That would be lovely," she replied as she, too, held out her hands. Off they went, the silver-haired one seemingly getting sprier and younger by the minute. As she and the Prince twirled and capered, he felt his own face losing wrinkles, his hair thicken and grow longer, his waist trimming.

Watching the elegant woman laughing in his arms, he thought,

"I must have been mistaken when I thought she was elderly." He noticed how her clothes, too, sparkled with flashes of gold and silver. She was altogether enchanting.

"May I have your name," Leon asked, as they paused a moment for the flute player to catch his breath.

Divine Love

"I am known as Lily. I am your Queen, risen from your heart by the Joy of our Creator's Love. We were always meant to be together—as eternal companions, and now, by God's Grace, we have met on this Earth in these physical forms."

As she spoke, a great shout floated across the air from the direction of the castle. "The people have returned," she said.

"Then, Queen Lily, let us depart," said, Leon as he took his Queen's hand gently. "Impetuous."

"Yes."

"Would you carry both of us, if it is not too much trouble?"

"Of course," replied his turquoise friend. "When a pure desire is released to the One, all is answered."

Leon and Lily climbed up onto the Unicorn's back and, holding his mane securely, got ready for a wonderful ride through the air.

"This is so much fun!" Lily called out as the Unicorn's huge wings lifted them into the sky. Leon enthusiastically agreed, and Impetuous turned his ears in reply.

High above the market they soared, over the forest, and down into the center of the castle courtyard.

What a different castle it seemed! All was a hustle and bustle of cooking smells, squawking chickens, rooting pigs, children running wild, people shouting at each other to *bring that quickly for the feast,* and *I'm coming. I'm coming.* When the Unicorn landed and Leon and Lily slid onto the packed earth, this was the signal.

A guardsman in red livery holding a golden trumpet blew a clear sound. The effect reminded Leon of the way a cloudy sky can clear to blue, all of a sudden, from a brisk wind.

"The King and Queen have arrived to celebrate the flow of Divine Love," the guardsman announced.

Leon and Lily looked at each other and smiled.

A girl of about twelve with long, dark hair, wearing a blue velvet gown, came up to them.

"Come to the hall," she urged. So Leon, Lily, and Impetuous crossed the courtyard and entered the Great Hall.

Everything had been magically transformed since the morning. A huge fire cracked and hissed in the fireplace.

Red cloths set with silver plates and cups adorned the tables. Richly-colored tapestries decorated the walls, woven with scenes of a turquoise Unicorn standing with a richly-clad Lady, surrounded by innumerable flowers and other plants.

"There you are again, Impetuous," Leon said, nodding at the intricate weavings. Impetuous only smiled and said,

"Follow me." He led them to the head of the table nearest to the door, near the warmth of the fire. For the first time, Leon noticed a small sack hanging around the Unicorn's neck. "Open this sack and look within," Impetuous told Leon and Lily. Leon pulled open the drawstring closure. They looked inside, amazed. Leon lifted out a necklace of gold entwined with silver, and covered with gems, while Lily did the same.

"Place them on each other." Impetuous spoke softly, yet his words echoed throughout the hall. Leon carefully placed the royal gems around Queen Lily's graceful neck. Lifting the other precious strand, Lily gave Leon a kiss on the cheek as she placed it on him. Impetuous, his mane and tail hanging down gracefully, his wings neatly folded against his sides, asked

"Are you ready to embrace your duties together as servants of the Love of God, promising to obey His Will forever and ever?"

"I promise to obey God's Will, always," said Leon.

"I, too, promise to obey God's Will always," said Lily.

"I am so grateful that God brought us together as eternal companions, to serve Him," she added, smiling at Leon, who returned her smile, saying gently,

"I am very grateful, too, my sweet Lily."

"Well, that's done, then," said Impetuous, a bit smugly.

"Thank you so much, Impetuous, for flying Leon here," Lily said, softly patting his turquoise mane.

"No problem," replied the Unicorn, bowing.

"Yes. I—we—are really grateful," Leon told him, feeling a bit overwhelmed. Turning to Lily, he asked, "Why don't we call your Mum and have her bring her household here, if that's acceptable to you, my Queen?"

"I'm sure she'd love to come," said Lily, smiling.

"I'd better send a messenger to Bridget also, and let my household know to travel here as well," Leon added.

"Good idea," said Lily.

"Excuse me." It was their friend the flute player from the market, along with his musical friends, their lute, a guitar, bells, and some hand drums. "We would like to help you celebrate!"

"That would be lovely," Lily told him as her husband nodded his assent.

Doors were propped-open to the courtyard, people appeared from every direction, and the music began. The newly-married King and Queen danced together under the moon-and-star-lit sky.

"How did all this happen?" Leon asked Lily as they danced together to tunes that sparkled with life. "First there was an empty castle and no Queen—now the castle is bursting with life, and the Queen blossoms with more and more beauty every moment." Leon looked at Lily, held her more closely, and thought of kissing her. Lily squeezed his hand and replied,

"I believe it must have happened through Divine Love. When the ever-present Love from our Creator, invisible as the wind and infinite as the sea, is allowed to flow through our hearts... all true desires are fulfilled."

Leon kissed his Queen. Lily kissed her King. The Love flowing from the All-Bountiful One cascaded between them, moving them like the people dancing to the waves of music echoing throughout the Castle, the torch lights swaying in the evening breeze, the Unicorn's hoofs clattering on the cobblestones, his broad wings moving powerfully as he lifted up into the night sky.

Looking up, the King and Queen saw him departing and waved, calling out in gratitude,

"Good-bye, Impetuous! We hope to see you again!" Already he was far, shining like a turquoise star. Faintly, the answer came floating down,

"See you again, when the need for Love is great, my friends."

More Stories to Read by the Authors of <u>The King and the Castle</u>

<u>www.loginthesoul.org</u> (Children)

<u>Andy Ant and Beatrice Bee</u>

<u>Beauty is on the Inside</u>

<u>Bee and Fairy Power</u> (a Short Novel in which the Beings of Nature use the super-power Virtue of Love to help humans Grow Organically)

<u>How Alexander the Gnome Found the Sun</u>

<u>Katie Caterpillar Finds Her Song</u>

<u>Return to Paradise</u> (a short novel in which Happy the Bluebird and Bright-Wings the Cardinal use Virtues to bring back Paradise)

For Adults:

www.loginthesoul.com (Adults)

Echoes of a Vision of Paradise: If you cannot Remember, You will return, Volumes 1 – 3

Echoes of a Vision of Paradise: If you cannot Remember, you will Return, a Synopsis

Restoring the Heart

The Simulator

Acknowledgment

We gratefully recognize the artists who contributed to Thinkstock, by Getty Images, allowing us to illustrate this book. Thank you.

Kito and Ling Productions—Copyright—July 2015

"Leon, you have a special destiny."

Color Leon

"My name is Impetuous, declared the Unicorn."

Color Impetuous

"The King and the Castle"

Color Me

"The King and the Queen"

Color Leon and Lily

"Know your destiny to fulfill."

Color the Old Man

Printed in the United States
By Bookmasters